TOMMY DONBAVAND'S FUNNY SHORTS

Viking Kong

WRITTEN BY TOMMY DONBAVAND
ILLUSTRATED BY LEO TRINIDAD

LONDON·SYDNEY

Franklin Watts
First published in Great Britain in 2016 by The Watts Publishing Group

Credits
Executive Editor: Adrian Cole
Design Manager: Peter Scoulding
Cover Designer: Cathryn Gilbert
Illustrator: Leo Trinidad

HB ISBN 978 1 4451 4673 7
PB ISBN 978 1 4451 4674 4
Library ebook ISBN 978 1 4451 4675 1

Printed in China

Franklin Watts
An imprint of
Hachette Children's Group
Part of The Watts Publishing Group
Carmelite House
50 Victoria Embankment
London EC4Y 0DZ

An Hachette UK Company
www.hachette.co.uk

www.franklinwatts.co.uk

Contents

Chapter One:
Born

OK, so I wasn't exactly there when the big lad was born. Only a few select women from the village were allowed into the actual royal birthing chamber. But I was in the room next door with his father, King Harald. And, by all the gods, it was noisy!

Queen Ingrid was yelling and screaming — mainly about King Harald by the sound of it. The king was seated opposite me, squirming every time he heard his name mentioned, usually accompanied by some kind of rude insult.

Then there was the chanting of the village shaman — the only man given access to the birthing chamber. He was dancing around, casting spells, sprinkling herbs and spraying potions.

Finally, the royal nurse was adding to the riot of sounds. She was shouting at the shaman for getting in her way and, if I heard correctly, "making the birthing chamber smell like the inside of a pair of berserker's pants".

By contrast, the people assembled in our room remained utterly silent. Normally we'd have been chatting and gossiping like villagers on market day, but, while we were in the presence of the king, we had to be invited to speak. Which is why there was no chatter to cover up the increasingly nasty abuse coming through the wooden walls from the queen.

It was all rather awkward.

So, I was delighted when Arvid, one of the villagers charged with keeping the fires lit, entered through the side door. He dropped his latest delivery of logs next to the hearth and sat beside me, eyes fixed in the direction of the birthing chamber.

"Hi, Erik," he whispered. "How's it going in there?"

"How should I know?" I replied.

Arvid shrugged. "Your sister's in there, isn't she?"

"Yes," I said slowly. "Freya is in there, but I'm not."

"But, you're twins..."

I blinked. "That doesn't mean I can see through her eyes, Arvid. We're two different people!"

Arvid's thick eyebrows met in the middle of his face as he frowned and tried to work this one out. For a moment, he looked as though he was genuinely in pain from the effort of thinking. Then he sniffed and wiped his hands on his tunic.

"So, twins can't—"

"No!" I snapped. "Whatever it is you're about to suggest, we can't do it!"

I quickly stopped talking as the king shot a glance in my direction. He didn't look happy, which may have been because I was speaking, but it could also have been because Queen Ingrid had just shrieked that he was a *veslingr,* or "puny wretch", that was never allowed within sight of her again.

Then we heard the one sound we'd all been waiting for — the cry of a newborn baby.

We all jumped to our feet, clapping and cheering. The king stood, blushing above his beard and rubbing his hands together nervously.

"Go on, Sire!" I said. "Go and see."

As King Harald walked towards the queen's chamber, the door crashed open and my sister hurried out. "Oh, excuse me, Sire!" she said with a bow. She stepped aside as the king strode inside to meet his first-born child.

"Freya!" I called, catching her attention. My sister rushed across the room and flung her arms around me.

"It's a boy!" she exclaimed.

"Is he healthy?" I asked.

Freya's eyes sparkled in the way they do whenever she's bursting to tell me something. "You could say that!" she giggled.

We've never had a family of our own, Freya and I. We lost our parents when the village was attacked by a rival Viking clan known as Hellfire. We were just toddlers. The rest of the community had rallied round to bring us up, and now we'd been given the chance to pay the clan back by helping to look after the royal baby. It was a very proud day for us both.

And here he was! Carried out of the birthing chamber by his proud father — who was struggling under the weight of a child the size of a small bull!

"He's a big lad!" I gasped.

Freya giggled again. "The biggest I've ever seen!"

"This is a proud day for the Poowiff Clan!" proclaimed the king. "For, today, born unto us is your future leader, whom I shall name Prince Olf!"

Then both the king and huge prince crashed through the floor. Freya and I hurried over to help hold the new arrival.

Instantly, the shaman leapt out of the

chamber and began to dance around us, chanting spells and scattering herbs ... until the royal nurse finally lost her temper and knocked him out cold with a single blow of her meaty fist.

Chapter Two:
Birthday

"Happy birthday toooo yoouuuuu!"

The entire village cheered as Prince Olf sat in the water of the bay, playing with his present — a life-sized Viking longboat.

It was hard to believe that two years had gone by since the young prince had been born, and even harder to believe how much he'd grown in that time...

When he was three months old, Olf stood as tall as his father, and was already too big to be lifted up by one person on their own — and that included the largest and strongest of the clan's warriors. So the royal staff had been doubled to help the king and queen look after their pride and joy.

A special, reinforced cot had been built for Olf to sleep in, and teams of seamstresses worked around the clock to stitch both new clothing and nappies for the ballooning baby.

At six months old, the tribe's farmers had given up filling troughs with milk to feed the prince. Instead, they simply led cows up to his side, allowing him to pick them up and drink straight from the udder.

By the time Olf's first birthday came around, he was too large to fit inside any of the village huts, so lengths of material were stretched across the trees in a nearby wooded area, and both Freya and I began to live outdoors with the prince.

And the less said about the day last spring
when we let him run around without a
nappy on for a while — and the resulting
wee-wee tsunami — the better.

Once we had heaved the birthday boy out of the water, the king and queen sat outside on their thrones and listened happily as Freya and I read Olf's greetings aloud.

"Greetings from the people of Tromsø!" I announced. "May Prince Olf continue to grow and be the pride of his clan!"

"And so he shall!" declared King Harald. "Although I won't mind so much if he doesn't listen to the 'keep growing' part."

"Best regards from Bergen," read Freya. "They have given Prince Olf the freedom of a city!"

Queen Ingrid frowned. "Don't you mean the freedom of *their* city?" she asked.

Freya examined the note again. "No, Your

Majesty," she said. "They've given him the freedom of Oslo instead. You may recall that, on the royal visit to Bergen earlier this year, your son sat on and destroyed their newly completed church..."

"Ah, yes," sighed the queen. "That poor, newly wed couple!"

"The greetings continue!" I cried. "This note comes all the way from..." I stopped and sniffed at the air. "Uh-oh," I said to my sister. "I think we may have a situation..."

I gave Freya a leg-up, and she climbed onto Olf's lap. "Phew!" she cried, pinching her nose. "Somebody needs changing!"

I pulled a horn from my belt and blew two sharp trills.

A moan went up around the village, but slowly everyone got to work. Teams of builders wheeled cranes into position, one of them led by Arvid.

"How much are we looking at?" he called over to me.

"Too early to say," I replied. "But he had three trees' worth of plums for breakfast this morning, so I'd be ready for anything!"

"Fair enough!" said Arvid. He turned to his team and gave the order: "Better get the big wheelbarrows!"

Carefully, Freya and I helped Olf to lie on his back — then one of his nurses climbed up and pulled out the old sword that served as a pin. Four others joined her to unfold the giant nappy, and everyone groaned again. This was a bad one!

"Heave!"

We looped ropes under Olf's arms, allowing the cranes to winch him up into the air — just enough for twenty gardeners

to scurry underneath and collect the
unpleasant contents of the nappy.

Not that anything would be going to waste
— all this stuff would be stored away and
used to fertilise crops in the future. The
clan already had enough fertiliser for the
next two hundred and eighty-five years.

Fully loaded barrows were wheeled away, allowing nurses with buckets and brooms to wash Olf. Finally, the old nappy was dragged down to the bay to be rinsed out. Then a replacement, made from stitched-together sails, was laid out underneath.

Olf was carefully lowered to the ground and the new nappy fastened. The large lad giggled as we helped him to sit up — just as his birthday cake was wheeled into view.

It was the size of a small lake with two burning trees in place of candles.

Prince Olf's face lit up at the sight of the treat. Taking a deep breath, he blew hard on the burning trees in front of him ... and set the entire village on fire.

Chapter Three:
Banished

It took three whole days and nights for
the flames to be entirely extinguished.
Afterwards, it was announced that the
clan had lost over three quarters of its
buildings, three longships and the forest had
disappeared almost halfway to the Great
Pine — a vast tree that towered even over
Prince Olf himself.

The village elders and the king gathered

together in the smoking remains of the great hall for an urgent meeting. Leaving Freya to play peek-a-boo with Olf, I snuck in through a burned-down doorway to listen in from behind a fresh pile of timber.

"The child is dangerous!" claimed one elder, an ancient former warrior with a beard that hung down past his knees. "He put the entire village, and the whole population, at risk!"

"Perhaps," countered King Harald. "But he didn't know what he was doing..."

"Which makes it all the worse!" barked another elder, this one bald. "At least when we were raided by Hellfire all those years ago, we had the right to defend ourselves. But we can't unsheathe our swords against the threat of a giant baby!"

"We don't have to," said Arvid's grandfather. "We could hold a blót to honour the gods. Just imagine the good luck it could earn us."

"No!" roared the king, jumping up. "I will not allow you to sacrifice my son!"

"Then, what is the alternative?" demanded Long Beard. "Wait until he farts and blasts us all out into the middle of the ocean?"

"Prince Olf grows bigger by the day!" declared Fluffy Beard. "It is only a matter of time before he causes death on an unimaginable scale — whether he means to or not. The only course of action open to us is to banish him from the tribe."

I clamped my hand over my mouth to stifle my cry of dismay.

"We could do that," said Grandad Arvid, "or we could hold the biggest blót ever seen — people would come from miles around..."

"Silence!" bellowed the king. "I cannot believe you are threatening to banish my only son out of the protection of this clan and into the wilderness. I will not allow it!"

"It is not your decision," Fluffy Beard

reminded him. "All judgements decided by the elders are put to the vote."

"I vote for the blót. It's a sacrifice I'm prepared to make for a bit of peace..."

"Quiet, you!"

The king took his seat and sighed. "Very well," he said. "It appears I have little choice in the matter."

Baldy Beard smiled kindly. "It is for his own good as well as ours, Sire," he said. "We wish your son no harm. Now, let us vote..."

It was a close call. I remained hidden and watched as each of the elders put forward their point of view and chose whether to banish Olf or have him remain with the Poowiff Clan.

In the end, the numbers were tied —
seven votes for each side.

"Then, we are at an impasse," said Baldy
Beard.

"Perhaps not," said Fluffy Beard. "King
Harald has yet to cast his own vote.
Whichever course of action he chooses will
resolve the matter once and for all."

Slowly, the king stood, suddenly looking
older and more tired than I had ever seen
him. "This is the hardest decision I have
ever had to make," he said. "But I have
to think of my clan, and not just my own
flesh and blood." He took a deep breath.
"I vote to banish Prince Olf from the
Poowiff Clan."

Seconds later, I was racing back across the smouldering village to where Olf and Freya were waiting. Tears stung my eyes as I ran. I couldn't believe the king had decided to send his son out into the wilderness all by himself.

I wasn't going to allow it! There was no way I would let Olf wander the forests and plains, scared and lonely. I had a plan.

It took me less than five minutes to explain everything to Freya. She was just as upset as I was, but agreed that there was only one course of action to take.

By the time the village elders arrived to make their announcement, Freya, Olf and I were long gone.

Chapter Four:
Blame

At first, life in the wild wasn't particularly difficult — it was even a bit exciting. We had told Olf that we were going on a trip to celebrate his recent birthday, and the titanic toddler had plunged deep into the forest willingly.

Grabbing what few belongings we could carry, Freya and I followed.

We stopped for a while at The Great Pine. Olf had never seen a tree bigger than himself before, and he danced around it, feeling the rough bark beneath his fingers.

I took the opportunity to discuss our situation with Freya. "If the clan is going to follow us, this is as far as they will come," I explained.

"Really?"

I nodded. "The lands beyond the Great Pine are poorly charted, and home to

vicious creatures such as wolves and bears."

Freya shuddered. "Will we be safe there?"

"We have to be," I replied. "We can't go back."

"Home," said Olf quietly.

Freya and I looked up to find Olf staring back down the valley, over the tops of the trees to where smoke was still rising from the village on the edge of the bay.

"His first word!" my sister exclaimed.

"Home!" said Olf again, louder this time.

I reached up and patted his knee. "Maybe one day," I said. "But first, let's go on an adventure!"

And so the three of us turned our backs on the clan, and strode into the unknown lands ahead.

The next few weeks passed by quite quickly, although we had to make certain changes to Olf's daily routine. We couldn't winch him up to change his nappies, so we used our sewing kit (one of the things we'd been able to stuff into our pockets before fleeing the village) and turned his existing nappy into a pair of pants.

Of course, this meant we had to start
potty training a huge toddler! Thankfully,
Olf got the idea reasonably quickly, and
we had very few accidents. Those we did
have were cleaned away by swimming
in sparkling rivers and under glistening
waterfalls.

Food was plentiful at first — there was

still fruit on the trees as we headed into autumn. Freya proved herself to be an expert survivalist — teaching both Olf and me which plants we could eat, and which would make us ill.

We slept out in the open but, as the days began to shorten and the temperatures fell, we were forced to seek out caves for shelter at night. This wasn't easy, as we started to come across wild animals who also wanted the same accommodation. More than once, we were forced to scare away a pack of wolves or a grizzly bear with our fiery torches. By the third week of our "adventure", Freya and I began to take turns keeping watch while Olf slept.

By day, Freya set about teaching Olf to speak — something he took to very swiftly. He soon learned the names of the natural elements surrounding us. But his favourite word was still the one place he couldn't go: home.

"Where King Daddy?" he asked me one day while we were gathering wood for a fire. "King Daddy gone."

"Not exactly," I said. "King Daddy is in the village. We're the ones who are gone."

"Go home," said Olf. "Go King Daddy, Queen Mummy."

I sighed. This wasn't going to be simple to explain. "We can't," I said. "Not now. Not today."

"Home soon?"

I nodded and smiled. "Home soon," I said.

That night, Freya and I sat by the fire as Olf snored away, half in and half out of the only cave we'd been able to find.

"You told him we'd take him home?" Freya questioned.

"I didn't know what else to say," I admitted. "I couldn't tell him that 'King Daddy' wanted to get rid of him, could I?"

Freya pushed a piece of edible, if tasteless, plant root onto the end of a stick and held it in the crackling fire. "I suppose not," she sighed. "I just don't want to get his hopes up, that's all."

After we'd eaten the little amount of food we'd been able to find that day, I took first watch while my sister leaned back against Olf's leg and closed her eyes.

I sat in silence as the fire burned down, wondering just how I was going to tell Olf that ... we ... YAWN ... couldn't ... Zzzzzz...

Chapter Five: Battle

"Erik! Wake up! Olf is missing!"

I jerked awake, my eyes stinging as they faced the bright light of dawn. Oh no! I'd fallen asleep when I was supposed to be keeping watch.

"What?" I croaked. "How can Olf be missing? You can't lose someone that size!"

But it was true. The beast of a baby had disappeared. Thankfully, the path he had taken through the trees was easy to follow.

Pausing only to grab our belongings, Freya and I gave chase.

"He must have heard us talking last night," my sister said as we ran. "He's heading back to the village."

"How?" I demanded. "He doesn't know where it is."

"He can see over the treetops, remember? All he has to do is spot the Great Pine, and head for that."

It turned out that Freya was right. For almost the entire day we followed the trail of destruction that could only be made by a giant, lumbering toddler. Finally, we found Olf at the foot of the Great Pine.

And, he wasn't alone.

"King Harald!" I said. "What are you doing here?"

"Looking for you!" the king replied. "And I'm so happy I've finally found you."

"Olf not happy!" said the big baby. "Olf sad with King Daddy!"

King Harald gazed up at his son in wonder. "You can talk!" he exclaimed.

The youngster bent to glare at his father. "Where Queen Mummy?"

"Yes, well — that's the thing," said King Harald, his cheeks flushing red. "It turns out that Ingrid, your mother, was not at all happy that I voted to, er ... ask you to move out. That's why I'm out here searching. I have been every day for weeks now."

Then Olf did something I'd never seen him do before: he reached down and picked up his father. The king was like a doll in his hand.

"Aargh!" the clan leader shrieked. "What are you doing?"

"See Queen Mummy!" said Olf, and he began to climb the Great Pine.

Freya and I called for the prince to come down, but he wouldn't listen. Higher and higher he clambered, with his terrified father clutched in his grasp.

Olf stopped near the top of the tree. His weight caused the trunk to sway back and forth alarmingly.

"Bad men!" cried Olf, peering down the valley towards the village. "Bad men make Olf cross."

King Harald stopped his screaming long enough to follow his son's gaze. "By the gods, he's right!" he gasped. "It's Hellfire! The village is under attack again!"

Olf slid down the Great Pine. He stomped through the forest and burst out from the trees, roaring like something from the Underworld! King Harald was still clutched in the toddler's hand, while both Freya and I clung on to him for dear life.

The Viking warriors from the Hellfire clan turned and fled back towards their ships — but they were not fast enough. Olf dropped off his passengers and thundered after the Hellfire warriors, crashing through burning buildings and kicking aside carts.

He caught up with the screaming stragglers at the mudflats, stomping several of the intimidated invaders into the soft ground. Then he waded out to sea, heading straight for our enemy's longships.

Arrows, axes, swords and more were hurled at the advancing attacker — all of them bouncing off his skin without leaving a mark behind.

"Bad men go away!" he bellowed, lifting

a couple of ships out of the water and smashing them together. The occupants fell back into the sea, all thought of conquering the Poowiff Clan long forgotten. The Vikings of Hellfire wanted just one thing now: to escape with their lives.

Olf raised a foot and pushed another ship down under the surface, grinding its mighty wooden beams to little more than dust on the seabed. Then he snatched up a fourth ship, tipped it upside down to empty out the crew, placed it on his head and beamed back towards the shore.

"Olf a Viking now!" he giggled.

The celebrations went on long into the night. There was food, drink, dancing and lots and lots of laughter for Prince Olf as he tottered about, thoroughly enjoying himself. Freya and I sat with the king and queen. We were special guests at their table as a reward for looking after their son in the wilderness. We laughed as the big little guy tried to keep the longboat balanced on his head as he danced.

In fact, things would have been perfect had the village shaman not decided to perform his self-created ceremony of victory for us all. You could almost feel the atmosphere of joy melt away as he began to chant and hop from foot to foot.

It didn't last long, however. Olf had stuffed himself with good food after several weeks of eating nothing but plants and berries, and the banquet wasn't sitting too well in his tummy.

The shaman was only a few minutes into his performance when Olf leaned forwards and threw up all over him.

I reckon they could have heard our cheers on the other side of the ocean.

THE END

TOMMY DONBAVAND'S FUNNY SHORTS

They'll have you in stitches!

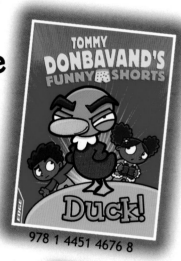

978 1 4451 4676 8

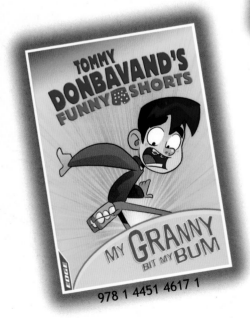

978 1 4451 4617 1

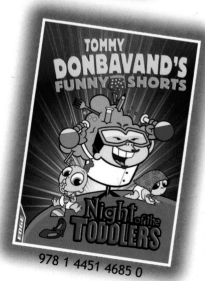

978 1 4451 4685 0